Dear Parents,

Welcome to the Scholastic Reader series. We have taken over 80 years of experience with teachers, parents, and children and put it into a program that is designed to match your child's interests and skills.

Level 1—Short sentences and stories made up of words kids can sound out using their phonics skills and words that are important to remember.

Level 2—Longer sentences and stories with words kids need to know and new "big" words that they will want to know.

Level 3—From sentences to paragraphs to longer stories, these books have large "chunks" of texts and are made up of a rich vocabulary.

Level 4—First chapter books with more words and fewer pictures.

It is important that children learn to read well enough to succeed in school and beyond. Here are ideas for reading this book with your child:

- Look at the book together. Encourage your child to read the title and make a prediction about the story.
- Read the book together. Encourage your child to sound out words when appropriate. When your child struggles, you can help by providing the word.
- Encourage your child to retell the story. This is a great way to check for comprehension.
- Have your child take the fluency test on the last page to check progress.

Scholastic Readers are designed to support your child's efforts to learn how to read at every age and every stage. Enjoy helping your child learn to read and love to read.

— **Francie Alexander**
Chief Education Officer
Scholastic Education

Another one for Julian
—T.J.

To Jules Arthur and Oliver Jamie
—J.H.C.

Text copyright © 1999 by Tony Johnston.
Illustrations copyright © 1999 by Judith Hoffman Corwin.
Activities copyright © 2003 Scholastic Inc.

Library of Congress Cataloging-in-Publication Data is available.

ISBN 0-439-09860-2

15 14 13 12 11 10 09   09 10 11 12 13/0

Printed in the U.S.A.   23
First printing, September 1999

BIG RED APPLE

by Tony Johnston

Illustrated by Judith Hoffman Corwin

Scholastic Reader — Level 1

Cartwheel
B·O·O·K·S ®

SCHOLASTIC INC.

New York   Toronto   London   Auckland   Sydney
Mexico City   New Delhi   Hong Kong   Buenos Aires

A tree grew.

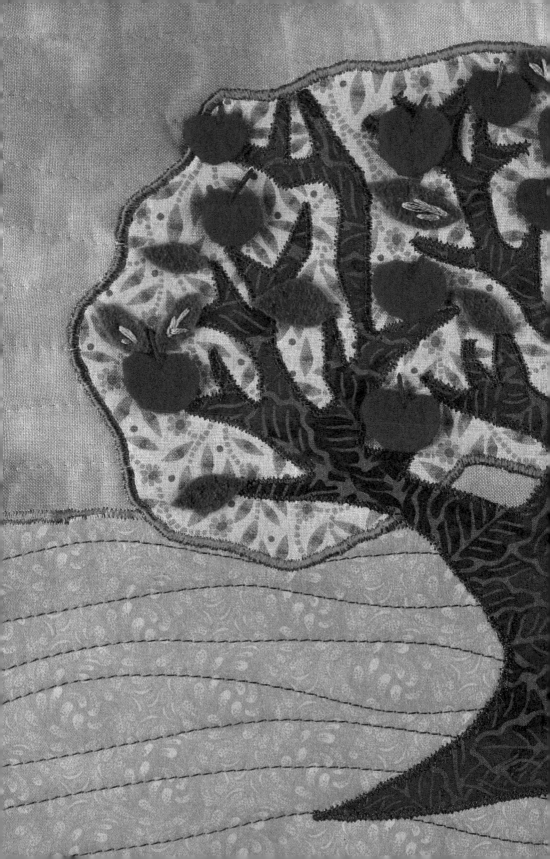

The tree was full of
big red apples.

Wind came.
It blew with a
big, loud
WHISPER!

It shook one big
red apple down.
The big red apple
lay on the ground
like a bright red rock.

A worm came.

Like a tiny mole,
it ate a tiny hole
in the big red apple.

A bird came.

It ate the worm
with a big loud
SQUAWK!

It pecked the big red apple. Then it flew off.

**A boy came.
He picked up the
big red apple.
THONK!
He slapped it in his hand
like a juicy red baseball.**

CRUNCH!
CRUNCH!
CRUNCH!
He ate the
big red apple.

So a tree grew.
The tree was full of
big red apples.

Sun came.
It shimmered and made
the seeds warm.

Rain came.
Its long, wet fingers
patted the seeds
into the dirt.

He spit the seeds.
PHUT!
PHUT!
PHUT!
The seeds fell
to the ground.
Phit!
Phit!
Phit!